Tangled

A M/F Friends-to-Lovers Sentient Object Romance

Yarn & Monsters

Book 3

Sabrina Cross

*For everyone who saw I had an octopus character
and has been harassing me for this book ever since.
I love you, you fucking weirdos.*

Author's Note

This is a sentient object romance. Humans will be getting it on with sentient objects. Don't worry, everyone is gleefully consenting.

If you read the last three sentences and think that's not for you, that's okay. There is still time to put this book down and walk away. No one will blame you. It's the sane thing to do.

But if you're going to stick around please be aware of the following: Graphic sexual activity (oral, vaginal, anal), sex with an inanimate object, use of sex toys, child abandonment, mild guardian abuse/neglect.

If you feel I am missing anything please reach out to me at authorsabrinacross@gmail.com and let me know. A complete list can be found at www.sabrinacross.com

Chapter One

"I want you to fuck me."

I jumped back as coffee sprayed across the small kitchen table and threatened to splatter me.

"What the hell, Jax?" I ran my hands over my dress to make sure I didn't get any stray drops on me.

"You can't just say shit like that." A purple and blue tentacle reached back to the counter and snagged the roll of paper towel. He used two more tentacles to clean up the coffee mess. I was thankful I had already packed my school bag and hung it by the door, or I'd have two dozen coffee-stained papers to hand back today. Not that the kids actually cared.

"I've thought about it, and it makes sense." I looked at the clock on the microwave and sighed. "I don't need an answer right now. I want you to think about it."

I walked past Jax to make my escape, but a

soft cotton tentacle wrapped around my wrist with surprising force.

"You can't just say something like that and walk out."

"I have to get to school." I tugged against his grip. A stuffed octopus shouldn't be able to hold me immobile, but the incubus demon possessing it maintained enough of his powers to do the seemingly impossible.

"Fern." Jax's voice was low with a hint of menace, but I wasn't afraid.

In the three months since Jax took possession of the octopus body, he'd done nothing overtly threatening or anything to make me afraid. Which was part of the reason I was asking him to help me.

Six months ago, my friends and I accidentally entered a deal with Lucifer. We had one year to fall in love or else he got our souls. As part of the deal, we were given demon guardians. According to them, they were here to guide and protect us, but I didn't buy it.

Especially not after Clover and Jasmine both fell in love with their assigned demon. It was actually rather insidious. Lucifer lost two unwilling victims and gained two people willing to follow their lovers into Hell.

I didn't, for one second, believe Clover or Jasmine wouldn't wind up there eventually. I didn't think even death would separate them from Candy or Phin.

Don't get me wrong. My friends were obviously loved, cared for, and spoiled by their demons. I didn't doubt that. I just thought it was a little convenient for Satan that they both happened to fall for their assigned demons.

It wasn't like that for Jax and I, though. We got on okay, but the lust demon had never so much as glanced at me sideways, let alone tried to seduce me. Honestly, it was kind of nice.

I was used to men only interested in me as someone to date or to fuck, not as a human. By comparison, having someone to hang out and play video games or watch TV with who didn't seem to see me as a woman, let alone someone he wanted. He was like a super considerate roommate I didn't particularly need or want.

Still, being the bare minimum of a decent human wasn't enough to tempt me into an eternity in Hell. I was still determined to find a human partner to fall in love with. But frankly, I was tired of being a twenty-seven-year-old virgin and I couldn't think of anyone better to teach me the ways of sex than a sex demon. He was literally made for it.

"Jax," I stared him down and his tentacle slowly released its grip on my wrist. "Look, think about it. We'll talk tonight. I'll pick up Chinese. But I'm going to be late."

I hurried away before he could grab me again. Putting it out there had taken all of my bravery for the morning.

Yes, I knew it was cowardly for me to toss it out there and run, but I really did want him to think about it. His knee-jerk reaction would be to tell me no because he wasn't interested in me that way. No need to face rejection first-hand.

After quickly slipping on my coat, I grabbed my tote bag and fled the apartment for school. Nothing was a better distraction than two dozen five-year-olds.

Chapter Two

"So, what did he say?" Violet asked, slipping into my classroom and closing the door behind her.

"Nothing. I kind of asked and ran." I continued writing the daily schedule on the board. I didn't want to see Violet's expression. I knew it would be nothing but disappointment.

"Fern, you're never going to get anywhere if you keep doing this." Her voice was kind, but she couldn't mask the exasperation. I exhausted her.

It was nothing new. Ever since the first day we became roommates, I had been exhausting Violet.

She hadn't been a fan of renting to someone nearly three years younger, assuming I'd slow them down. Seven years later, she still didn't understand why I did most of the things I did. But we were friends, and in her own Violet way, she loved me.

Still, while Violet and her friends had been

one of the best things that had happened to me, Violet was also the one who had cursed us. She'd roped us all into doing what we'd thought was a true love spell but was actually a signed and sealed devil's bargain.

So really, it was a toss-up if I wanted to hug her or strangle her most days. Luckily for her, I wasn't prone to violence.

"I told you; I asked him. I just want to give him time to process. Okay?"

"Fern, he's a literal sex demon. He's not going to turn you down. Hell, I'm shocked he made it this long without sexual energy to feed on. He should have withered away and died with the Sahara, that is your sex life."

Yes, incubus demons fed on sexual energy. Yes, I had probably been starving Jax for three months. I wasn't like Violet. I couldn't just take some random guy from the bar home. It wasn't in my make-up.

I spun around to glare at her, glancing to make sure the door was still closed.

"Chill, still twenty minutes before the doors open," Violet said. She stood on the far side of my desk with her hands on her wide hips. It was her annoyed stance. Which might be more threatening if she wasn't five-two at best.

Violet was short and curvy, with the personality of a Doberman. She was a solid four inches shorter than me. Her hair was currently pastel pink and tied up in a messy knot on the top of her head. Honestly, physically and personality wise, we couldn't be more different, but somehow, we worked.

"Are you seeing Braden tonight?" I asked, changing the subject.

Violet and I had been hitting the bars and singles events trying to meet someone to love. So far, only Violet had met anyone worth a real first date.

"Yeah, big third date." She shrugged and dropped her hands from her hips. "I don't know. I like him, but it feels like something is missing, you know?"

Honestly, I didn't. There was a reason I was a twenty-seven-year-old virgin. My contact with the opposite sex was limited and very often negative.

"So, what now?" I asked. We had six months to find love. Not a lot of time to sit and see if things develop.

"We're not exclusive. You and I can keep looking. In the meantime, I'll keep dating him and see how it goes." She shrugged again, but I could see the stress on her face. It was there in the tightness around her eyes and the pinch of her mouth.

We were running out of time and no one felt it more keenly than Violet. The one who got us into this mess and the only one with a hope of finding a way out of it. She spent all of her free time looking for ways to escape our bargain and free us. A part of me would probably always be angry at Violet, but I couldn't blame her.

She had thought it was a joke, just as the rest of us had.

"I'd better get to class. If I don't see you, call me this weekend and let me know how it goes with Jax."

"Yeah, will do." Would absolutely not do. "Have fun with Braden. Make sure you're giving him a real chance. He seems nice and might be good for you."

"Yeah, yeah," Violet grumbled as she headed out the door.

Time lost all meaning that day and by lunch, I was filled with regret and embarrassment over how I had propositioned Jax at the breakfast table. I should have waited and let him reject me and just taken the hits of his reaction. This waiting and wondering was agony.

By the time I finally packed up, I was seriously debating just never going home again.

I sat in the apartment parking lot trying to come up with the gumption to go inside for twenty minutes. After that, the frigid February cold told me I had to either go inside or possibly freeze to death.

What had I been thinking? Why had I just blurted that out and left myself nine hours to wonder about his reaction?

Obviously, morning Fern was a lot braver or more reckless than evening Fern.

Jax was waiting for me when I finally opened the door. He stood on four tentacles, his rounded body about six feet in the air. Two sets of tentacles braced on the doorway separating the entryway from the rest of the apartment.

"I was about to come drag you inside."

I laughed. I couldn't help myself. The image of a giant crochet octopus hauling me across the frozen parking lot was hysterical. Oh, what would the neighbors think?

"I'm glad hypothermia amuses you," he growled. "Avoiding me?"

I sobered and anxiety slammed back into me like a brick. Nope. Was not ready to talk about it yet.

"Long day." I set my bags down to shrug off my coat and tug my boots off. "I'll have to warm up the food."

I reached for the bags, but purple and blue tentacles got there first.

Jax carried dinner and my tote through the apartment to the kitchenette dining area. I took a shaky breath and followed.

"Cold Chinese is better anyway," Jax said. He opened a carton and brought it to his face.

I still hadn't figured out the mechanics of how he ate and drank. There had to be a level of magic involved. Somehow, he consumed food without staining his cotton yarn, or making a mess on the floor.

I watched him for a moment before moving to the table and grabbing my chicken and rice. Normally, the silence between us was comfortable, but it was now tense and heavy. I struggled to eat with the weight of it.

"Are we talking about it yet?" Jax asked, when I was halfway through my meal. I nearly jumped as he broke the silence.

"Nope." I kept my gaze on my meal, and hoped he would drop it.

Of course he didn't. Damn demon.

"You asked me to fuck you," Jax said, setting his carton aside.

"Technically, I didn't ask. I just said I wanted you to. I changed my mind. We never have to talk about this again."

I got up and headed to the kitchen for a drink. There was a bottle of wine chilling in my fridge and calling my name.

"Pretty sure we do," Jax said, following me into the kitchen. It was cramped and the two of us in there left very little room to avoid touching each other.

"I'm not going to fuck you, Fern," Jax said.

I struggled not to wince.

"Great. Fine. Glad we cleared that up." I pushed past him and went to the living room with my bottle of wine and a glass. I was absolutely drinking the whole bottle.

"We're not done." Jax followed behind me. "Why don't you tell me what it is you really want?"

"I told you." I poured wine into the glass. "We're not talking about it."

A tentacle wrapped around the glass and pulled it from my hand. I yelped in surprise and bit back a growl.

Fine. Whatever. I still had the bottle.

I was mid-drink when Jax pulled the bottle from me as well. Except this time, he managed to spill it all over my dress.

"Damn you!" I launched to my feet and stomped to my bedroom.

"You started this sweetness. And we're not doing it while you're drunk."

"We're not doing this at all." I slammed my door in his face. It didn't lock and even if it did, it wouldn't keep him out. It was a juvenile move. But damned if it didn't feel good.

I had barely crossed my room before the door slammed open behind me and banged into the wall. I swung around to watch Jax come through, his movements determined as he marched towards me on four tentacles.

At first, it had been so ridiculous to see him walking about. I'd spent most of the first month trying not to laugh, but now it was just normal. And how messed up was it that a six-foot-tall octopus walking on four legs was my new normal?

"I don't want to fight with you." Tentacles gently but firmly circled my wrists, keeping me in place. "You just don't know what you're asking."

"I'm not asking for anything." I yanked against him, but he didn't budge. "It was a moment of insanity, okay? A crazy moment fueled by Violet, and tequila and I just want to forget I said anything."

"You've waited twenty-seven years to have sex." Jax brushed a loose strand of hair over my shoulder with a free tentacle. The move was oddly sweet and just fueled my anger and frustration. I didn't want him sweet. I just wanted someone who actually respected me to touch me. "Why would you want your first time to be with something like me?"

That one I did have an answer to. A few answers. Though most of them didn't make as much sense and seemed weak now.

"Who better for my first time than a sex demon?"

"Sweetness, I'm a giant yarn octopus. I can't give you what you're asking for."

"That's not what I've heard." The grip around my wrists tightened and then let go. I stumbled backward until I was sitting on my bed.

"I can't exactly give you my cock, now can I?"

I snorted at him. "There are more ways to fuck than using your penis, and of all people you should know that."

"It's not the same."

"Obviously." I glared at him. "I'm a virgin, not an idiot or innocent."

"Virgins, innocents, they're pretty much the same." A soft tentacle slid down my leg and wrapped around my ankle. I kicked him off.

"If all it took to have sex was to shove something in a vagina, I wouldn't still be considered a virgin. But no, solo play doesn't appear to count and frankly, I don't want to go to Hell a virgin. Seems like a total waste."

Silence fell between us after that massive over share. I flopped back on the bed and dragged a pillow over my face.

After a moment that felt like an eternity, I felt Jax's tentacles land on my legs just below the hem of my skirt and just above my knees.

"You're right, sweetness," Jax said quietly. "There are a lot of ways to get fucked."

I flung the pillow away when I felt him slide my damp dress up my legs. I sat up so quickly I nearly knocked him over.

"What are you doing?"

"Giving you what you want." He inched my dress higher but stopped when he met resistance from where I was sitting on the skirt.

"You said you're not going to fuck me." I shifted up, the movement loosening the skirt beneath me. "And I told you I changed my mind, anyway."

"You haven't." Another set of tentacles followed the path of the first, blazing a warm trail up my bare thighs. My heart started racing in my chest when the skirt finally bunched at my waist, exposing the very tops of my thighs.

"You're a liar," Jax whispered. "And I'm not going to fuck you."

His tentacle point reached the apex of my thighs, and I wasn't sure if I wanted to snap my legs closed or open them to give him better access.

It turned out it didn't matter. Before I could decide, he retreated, pulling all limbs away from my body.

"Take off your dress."

I hesitated. It was just a beat, but long enough to change Jax's languid tone to hard and demanding.

"You want to get fucked by someone other than yourself? Take the dress off."

With shaking hands, I pulled the damp sweater dress up over my head and held it in front of me. I tried to cover myself with the material, but Jax was having none of it.

His tentacles came back to me, smoothing up my arms, down my calves, across my collar bone before dipping down to trace the tops of my breasts. My breath caught in my throat as my body burned under his touch. I didn't even notice when the dress pulled free of my hands.

Just as suddenly as his touch came, it stopped. He leaned back again and sat propped awkwardly on two limbs.

"You have a toy. Get it." Again, I hesitated. A sharp slap landed on my hip. Not violent or painful but enough of a jolt to prod me to move. I reached into my bedside table and grabbed the rabbit I had stored there.

I tried to offer it to Jax, but he shook his body no and leaned further back.

"I'm not going to touch you. I'm going to sit right here and watch as you get yourself off. You want to have sex? First, you need to get comfortable with your body and pleasure."

I knew damn well that wasn't true. How else would you explain all of the fumbling teenage sex being had?

As if reading my mind, Jax pinned me with a stern look. "Any man can shove his dick into a hole. You have to be comfortable enough with yourself to demand what you like and what gets you off."

"But do I have to do that with an audience? I'm pretty well-versed in what gets me off."

"Sure, you are. But can you do it with another person?"

Breaking his declaration not to touch me, Jax used two tentacles on my shoulders to lay me back on the bed. Once I was down, he slid them down my body, along the outer curve of my breast, down my sides, over my hips until they rested on my knees. With a little force, he pried my thighs apart and inserted his body between my legs. I couldn't close them without squishing him.

"Touch yourself, sweetness."

Chapter Three

Was I actually going to do this? I wasn't totally inexperienced, but some teenage fumbling or drunken groping wasn't nearly the same as this.

Jax sat braced between my legs, his tentacles holding my legs open. The light was dim, but he would be able to see every inch of me.

I'd never been so exposed in my life.

"It's your choice, sweetness." Warm tentacles slid across the outside of my thighs and down my calves. "We can stop right now."

"No." I turned the insertable part of the vibrator on with trembling hands. I closed my eyes and brought the toy between my legs to gently brush against my vulva. It was a tease and a jolt of feeling at the same time. I ignored the feeling of Jax's eyes on me. I ignored the tentacles on my knees, and those wrapped around my ankles.

I wouldn't be able to do it if I thought too hard about his presence, but I'd used that toy dozens of times and knew how to wield it to get myself off. Years of friendship with Violet and Clover had taught me sexual independence and how to care for my own needs when I wasn't willing to risk it with a man. The rabbit wasn't the only toy I owned.

I kept brushing the rounded head of the vibrator against me gently, winding myself up. I briefly wondered if Jax would have chosen a different toy if he knew about the chest of them under my bed. My eyes flew open and met his.

His eyes focused on my face, rather than what I was doing between my spread thighs. There was an intensity to his expression that I couldn't read, but it sent a flash of heat through me and made me feel brave.

Reaching down with my other hand, I tugged my underwear to one side and moved the rabbit to touch my skin. The change in intensity had my hips thrusting up against it. Jax chuckled, low and deep and dirty.

I closed my eyes again.

"You're too tense," he admonished. "Just relax and feel it. Let the pleasure take you."

I took a deep breath and tried to do what he said. It was impossible to forget he was there with the weight of him between my splayed legs, but I did my best as I moved the toy up to brush against my clit. The vibrations were an instant jolt of pleasure. Tentacles came to my hips to hold me in place as I brushed the head of the toy over my clit again and again.

Suddenly, there was pressure around my waist for a moment just before a rending sound tore through the room. I jolted upright just as Jax tugged the front of my underwear down and away from me.

"What the fuck?"

"Just giving you some more room." He grinned and I wanted to kick him. It must have shown on my face because his grip around my ankles tightened.

"I liked these underwear!"

I'll buy you more," he promised. I grumbled, all pleasure gone in my annoyance.

"I can't believe you did that." I pointed the vibrator at him and shook it.

He eyed the pink and white toy and I flushed, realizing how ridiculous I must look. I yanked the still-vibrating toy back toward my chest. "Sorry."

Jax laughed, "I can't say I've ever been threatened with a vibrator before. The other demons may never take me seriously again."

"Keep it up and I'll make you a hole to shove it in."

"Fuck, that's vicious. It's kind of hot." Tentacles landed on my shoulders and pushed, knocking me back onto the bed. "Now stop stalling and play with that pretty pussy until you come."

My entire body went hot. With my underwear in tatters, Jax had a front row view of my exposed sex. I was hyper-aware of how my lips were slightly spread and the dampness that gathered from my teasing touches.

Instinctively, my legs tried to close, but Jax was still between my thighs so all I could do was press against the sides of him. While he was technically a stuffed toy and should have been easy to squish, something about the demon possessing it gave the stuffed octopus density and form that shouldn't have been possible. So instead of closing my legs tightly, it felt like I was pressing against a basketball between my thighs. There was no way to close my legs.

"Come on, sweetness. You wanted this. Touch yourself for me. Let me hear what you sound like when you come. I want to know how sweet you smell when you let go." Tentacles exerted pressure against the inside of my knees, spreading my thighs wide.

My face was flaming, and I was certain my entire body was turning red in a blush when I nodded and brought the toy back to myself. This time I circled it around my opening before bringing it back up to my clit. I was damp but nowhere ready to insert it. There was no way I was stopping to get lube. If I paused, I knew I would chicken out.

Pleasure arced through my body to coil low in my belly as I teased my sensitive clit with the rounded head of the toy. I reached down with my free hand to flick on the "ears" of the rabbit toy.

When I lined it up at my entrance, the tentacles around my ankles and on my thighs tightened almost painfully. Briefly I wondered what Jax was thinking, but I wasn't brave enough to ask him. Instead, I pressed the toy inside me until the ears wrapped around my clit.

"Oh my god!" I moaned, thrusting my hips up. Pleasure pooled low in my belly as I moved the toy slowly in and out.

It only took moments before the pleasure coiled tight, making every muscle in my body tense. My thighs shook under Jax's weight and I was so, so close. It never took much to make me come; but this was fast, even for me.

"That's it, sweetness. Let go." Jax's voice was a growl. The sound of it sent a thrill through me. "Come for me, Fern."

The coil snapped, and I moaned as my inner muscles tightened almost painfully around the silicone toy. I rode it out, thrusting my body against the air. Pleasure shuddered through me and left me trembling on the bed as it faded.

"Mmmm, so pretty." Jax cooed. He brushed a tentacle down the crease where my thigh met my body and I twitched under the sensation. I moved to pull the toy out and turn it off, but a tentacle landed over my hand. "Do it again."

"I can't," I whined, trying to scoot away from the tentacle tracing my crease over and over. The movement was a weird combination of ticklish and arousing, and my overstimulated body couldn't handle it.

Jax nudged the vibrator deeper inside of me and I jolted, my back arching off the bed as the toy brushed against my cervix. I knew a lot of people weren't a fan of the feeling, but there was a kind of pleasurable pain that happened every time I hit mine. It was intense and left my brain and body confused and panting.

"There's a good girl." He brushed my hand away and took control of the toy. Slow, deep thrusts had me clenching the white quilt beneath me. Panting as pleasure washed over me again. The dull ache of pain that came with him pushing against my cervix was a sharp counterpoint to the vibrations fluttering around my clit. Heat suffused me as he pressed in deep and held it there.

"Too much," I panted, reaching down to push him away. Instead, I found my wrist encircled by a tentacle and pinned to the bed. "Please, it's too much."

Pressure and pleasure like I'd never experienced before was built inside me. It left my muscles trembling and weak as I worked my hips against the toy. I wasn't sure if I wanted more or needed it to stop. My inner muscles were so tense it ached.

"You can take it." Jax pressed a little deeper, and I groaned. "Just one more. You can do that for me, can't you, sweetness?"

"No. No, no, no. Can't." But even as I said it, my body was arching and the tight coil of tension broke as an orgasm crashed through me. My body folded in on itself as my muscles milked the toy.

Slowly, Jax worked the vibrator out of me and

turned it off. I relaxed against the bed, my muscles weak and liquid. I was too sated to care that my legs were still splayed and I was on full display.

Something nuzzled against my leg and I found the strength to lift my head and look down my body to see Jax rubbing the side of his face against my thigh.

"I thought you weren't touching me." I dropped back down, completely spent.

"I lied." He wrapped his tentacles around my legs and shoved so that they were on the bed. He then took the blanket I kept folded over the footboard and brought it up over me.

I shifted, so I was laying properly and yawned.

"I couldn't help myself. You are positively delicious when you come for me."

Somehow, despite everything we'd just done, I could feel myself blushing. Jax brushed a tentacle across my cheek, which I knew had to be bright red.

"Get some sleep, sweetness."

Before I could even reply, he was across the room and out the door. I wrapped the blanket tighter around me, and told myself it didn't matter. That there was no part of me that wished he would stay.

Chapter Four

"And don't forget, next Friday is our Valentine's Day mixer. We encourage both couples and singles of all ages to attend. We have activities planned for the kids and will be serving light refreshments." Pastor David was too chipper. He wasn't bad looking. Probably late thirties, dark blond hair, a rounded face with blue eyes and generally happy. He rocked a dad bod but wasn't overweight. Just a little soft.

He was typically upbeat but nobody, especially not a widower like him, should be that excited about a church-sponsored Valentine's Day party.

Something of my feelings must have shown on my face because there was a sharp pinch to my thigh as my grandmother sent me a discreet glare. I bit back a yelp and did my best to school my features into a blank expression. I was too tired to present a happy face but I could manage a neutral.

The pastor wrapped up the service and people started gathering their things and making their way out of the sanctuary. As always, Grandmother and I remained in our pew in the second row until the sanctuary was nearly empty. Grandmother liked to avoid the crowds. The only exception to this was when Grandmother was on refreshment duty and we left in the last moments of the service to prepare.

Church had always been a duty for me. I wasn't entirely sure what my relationship with God was most days. And lately, since I started rooming with a demon, I had been further from Him than ever. But whatever my feelings about church, religion, or God were, every Sunday I sat in the pew for the early service with my grandmother.

"You will be helping with refreshments for the event, yes?" Grandmother said. I shifted to look at her. This was the first I was hearing of it.

"I hadn't planned on going. Some friends and I were planning on getting together."

She tsked, her face becoming even more pinched. I mentally closed my eyes and sighed. I knew that face. Nothing ever good came from that face.

"Don't you think it's time to find yourself a good man and settle down? You're nearing spinsterhood."

"I'm twenty-seven!"

"Yes, and how many years do you have left to bear children?" She picked up her bible and slid it into its special sleeve before putting it into her large handbag. I tucked my bible into my tote bag, not bothering with the book sleeve that was floating around in there somewhere.

"I'm not even sure I want children." This time I did yelp when Grandmother's surprisingly strong fingers pinched my thigh.

"What kind of attitude is that? Who is going to want you if you won't provide them with heirs?" Good God she sounded like a mother from a historical romance novel. Spinster? Heirs? No, thank you.

It was no wonder I wasn't ready to hop on the mommy train. My own had abandoned me as a toddler, leaving me to be raised by my grandmother, who was hardly a warm and caring person. I loved kids, but honestly, I didn't think there were any good mom genes in our family. I really did not want to have my own and learn I was just as terrible as the rest of the women in my family.

No, it was safer to enjoy the kids in my classroom and leave parenthood to other people. Better people. People who weren't likely to give their children years of trauma to unpack with their therapist.

"I will try to drop in for a bit, but I already have plans. If you needed my help with refreshments, you should have asked sooner." Almost as soon as the words were out of my mouth, I wanted to snatch them back. I've been working on setting boundaries for years, but every one I set was still a struggle.

"I don't know what I did to deserve such an ungrateful child." She got up and hefted her black purse over her shoulder. The white button down and black slacks were still as perfectly pressed as when we arrived over an hour ago. Wrinkles wouldn't dare to muss Grandmother's clothing. Her silver hair was short and curly around her face. She was in her mid-seventies but age hadn't slowed her down a bit.

I sighed and followed after her. I stopped in the coatroom to get our things before seeking her out, using the moment in the dim room to take a few deep breaths and calm myself before I did something I would regret. Like strangling the old woman.

I found Grandmother near the refreshment table, talking to Pastor David. He held a styrofoam cup of coffee in his hand. Grandmother had nothing. She wouldn't drink from a styrofoam cup if she was dying of dehydration. It was crass.

"Ahh Fern, I was just telling Pastor David that you won't be able to assist us Friday night." Grandmother said, her voice sweet. I swallowed to relax my jaw before I ground my teeth to nothing. "Kids these days, always too busy for the church."

"Fern is hardly a child." Pastor David offered me a bright smile. I smiled back, but I wasn't sure it wasn't just a feral baring of my teeth. "I'm sorry to hear you won't be able to join us at the party. I was hoping you'd save a dance for me."

So, here's the thing about Pastor David, he's

been the pastor at our church for three years, ever since his wife died from complications from her last pregnancy. He came with his three small children who were basically hellions. In those three years I have not been able to determine if he's actually flirting with me or if his normal friendliness comes across flirty. Usually when I interact with him, we're with the old folks or the kids and I just cannot tell.

He doesn't give off the ick vibes I get from a lot of men, but it was still weird.

"I wish I would have known I was needed earlier." I struggled not to glare at Grandmother. "Unfortunately, I've made plans with my girlfriends and it would be rude to back out at this point. I'm sure everyone will have fun without me."

There was a beat of awkward silence and I tried to figure out a way to make my escape without being rude.

Grandmother placed her hand on Pastor David's arm and smiled. "If Fern can't come to you, maybe you should take her out dancing. The poor girl doesn't get out much."

Did she just?

To the pastor?

"Grandmother!" I snapped, completely mortified at my grandmother trying to play matchmaker. "I'm sure Pastor David has better things to do."

This time I knew my smile was a baring of teeth rather than any sort of actual smile. I grabbed my grandmother around the upper arm and tugged her toward the door and my escape from this humiliation. Pastor David settled his free hand on my shoulder, stopping me.

"That sounds like it could be a lot of fun." His hazel eyes were bright as he looked down at me.

Oh God, oh God, oh God.

The last thing I wanted was to go dancing with the pastor. I was perfectly happy seeing the man for a couple of hours on Sunday. Not only that, but he was a single dad and his kids were terrible. They were practically feral. I'd actually embrace my one-way ticket to Hell if it was a choice between being their step-mom or the fire and brimstone.

My brain was panic-flailing inside my head. It's the only excuse I have for what came out of my mouth. "I'm sorry. I'm seeing someone."

Pastor David practically deflated in front of me. Grandmother's eyes narrowed in a deep glare. I wasn't sure if it was because I ruined her matchmaking plans or because I might, possibly, be dating someone she didn't know about.

"Oh, that's too bad," Pastor David said, sounding dejected. It was a little sad, really.

"Since when?" Grandmother demanded.

"It's new." More panic-flailing brain panic. "We're still learning each other and seeing if it's worth pursuing."

I yanked on my coat and draped Grandmother's over her shoulders. I needed to get out of there before I did more damage. Now I had another reason to find someone to date, and fast. I'd hate to face Grandmother's wrath if I didn't produce a man in the next few weeks.

"Anyway, great sermon today, Pastor David. Have a nice week!" I leaned over and pressed a quick kiss to Grandmother's cheek. "Grandmother, I'll call you later. Drive safe."

And with that, I made my escape.

What the hell had I just done?

Chapter Five

I was still fuming when I got home. My embarrassment turned into rage at the audacity of my grandmother. How dare she?

She had done a lot of questionable things over the years. I'd never had much freedom as a child. I was used to her controlling my life and I'd spent the last seven years learning to break that habit. But this was too much.

"How was church? Any sign of God?" Jax asked from his perch on the couch. He was leaning against the arm with his tentacles spread all akimbo, taking up the entire space.

"No, but are you sure my grandmother isn't a demon?" I plopped down next to Jax, not caring I was sitting on two of his tentacles. He should have moved them if he didn't want me sitting on him.

"I think I'd like to meet this woman." The tone wasn't friendly.

I was kind of tempted to see who would come

out on top in a demon versus grandmother show-down. Except I was somewhat afraid it would be Grandmother.

"What did she do this time?"

"Tried to set me up with the pastor." I shook my head and reached for the remote. There was no way I was going to sit through some sort of sports-ball game on top of today's humiliation. "The man is at least ten years older than me and he's the pastor. It's all kinds of weird."

I brought up my favorite streaming service and began scrolling through, looking for some-thing to let me forget about the foot hanging out of my mouth.

"He could be your one, though. Why not give him a chance?" Jax prodded my shoulder with one tentacle, the move comfortable and friendly. I smacked him away. "You're running out of time."

"Don't remind me." I found one of my com-fort movies and turned it on, trying to sink into the English countryside.

A tentacle wrapped around my shoulder and hugged. It was the most affection Jax had shown me in the nearly three months he'd been there. I wondered if he felt bad for me or if it was because of what I'd done on Friday.

We hadn't talked about it. A part of me was desperate to talk it out, wanted to know if we'd ever do it again. Another part of me, the bigger part of me, was terrified to bring it up. I didn't want to hear that it was a mistake or that he re-gretted touching me.

Still, I wasn't going to turn down a hug. No matter what motivated it. I was in a perpetual state of touch-starvation and not prepared to turn down any sort of affection.

"Reminding you is why I'm here." Jax's voice was gentle. So was the tentacle he brushed over my hair and down my arm. He was being so gentle with me; I was afraid I was going to start crying. And if I started, I wasn't sure when I would stop.

"Can we pretend for just one day that I don't have a death sentence looming over my head? I don't have a rigid and cold grandmother, I'm not unworthy of love, I'm not the scared little virgin girl? For one day, can I just be Fern?"

Tears were a pressure behind my eyes. It matched the pressure in my chest. More tentacles wrapped around me, circling me in soft, yarny limbs. I sank into the warmth and feeling of being held.

"You can be whoever you want." Jax nuzzled his head against me and some of the pressure in my chest gave way. "But Fern?"

"Yes?"

"I don't ever want to hear you say you're unworthy of love again. You are warm, and kind, and deserve to be loved."

I nodded, but I didn't agree with him. Why else would my mom have left me and never looked back? Why else would I still be single and a virgin at twenty-seven? I had never been waiting for marriage. I just wanted someone to love me first. And no one had been capable of it. There was something broken inside of me and nothing I did could fix it.

That was the thing my friends couldn't understand. And frustrated Jax so much. I'd never find my true love because I wasn't worth loving. I was just trying to enjoy what was left of my life before I was dragged to Hell.

There was no escaping the flames.

Not for me.

Chapter Six

I decided to say fuck it to all responsibilities and just take the day off. Laundry would always be there. I could eat simple meals instead of prepping stuff. The five-year-olds didn't care about getting their papers back so there was no rush to stamp and sticker a hundred alphabet tracing sheets and coloring pictures.

I also realized I could never return to church. I wasn't sure I could ever look Pastor David in the face again, knowing he wanted to date me. A part of me was okay with that. My faith had always been a shaky thing, and I got little from church. I went to appease my grandmother, but this was another boundary I would need to lay down. She humiliated and embarrassed me and I would not forget that.

"I'm begging you; can we do something with explosions or car races or, oh, what about a slasher film? I could really go for some blood right about now." Jax begged, as I scrolled to find the next movie in my marathon.

After the first movie, a historical romance, I changed out of my church clothes and threw my hair up in a loose bun. The second and third movies were rom coms. We'd watched them while decimating my bottle of wine, a bag of popcorn, and my chocolate chip stash. We had a pizza on order and I was trying to figure out what to watch next.

"I'm not big on all that blood and gore stuff. It's kind of gross. I don't know how you watch it."

"I'm a demon, sweetness. Cornstarch blood isn't going to bother me."

Oh. Right. Demon, Hell, torture and torment. Makes sense.

The mix of food in my stomach wasn't settling so well. That was my future. A life of torture and torment.

I wondered if Jax would be the one to dole it out. Or if he'd be in trouble because he failed to find me a husband. Would they torture him, too? Would it hurt?

"No horror," I snapped out, before turning on another fluffy rom com. Jax groaned but didn't argue. Instead, he let me snuggle into him and wrapped his tentacles around me.

"What's wrong?" He asked, after a few minutes, gently rubbing my back. I wanted to scream at him for being so nice to me.

I didn't want him to be nice to me. He was just another sign I was unlovable. He was a sex demon and even he wouldn't touch me. He was just part of the plan to get my soul to Hell. He was my damnation.

I could have said any of that. I could have brushed it off as I brushed off my feelings too many times before. I could have said anything else. Instead, I had to ask the question that wouldn't stop burning its way through me.

"Why won't you touch me?" His movements stopped and the firm warmth of him withdrew. "What is it about me that turns everyone off?"

"It's not about you." His voice was even, neutral. I hated it. "There is nothing wrong with you. You're perfect."

"Right. A perfect pretty little doll to be left on the shelf, too precious to play with." I shoved away from him and jumped up, needing to move. The apartment was a decent size, but it felt too small as I paced the space.

"Is that what you want, Fern? You want to be played with?" Now his voice was low, dangerous. "Months of dating nice, human men. Years of dating them, and now you want to be touched by me?"

He lifted his tentacles, showing off his lack of hands. He reached out to touch me, but pulled back. "You want this? This is what you want? This farce of a form?"

"I want you!" It wasn't until the words were out that I realized how true they were. I wanted him. I wanted the demon behind the silly crochet form. I didn't think about the fact he wasn't human. I didn't care that he was just a little ridiculous in his current form.

I wanted Jax.

"I'm a fucking demon, Fern. You don't seem to be able to remember or understand what it means. You think everything I do is like this? Babysitting a little idiot who got herself into a mess with upper management? I've done things that would make your skin crawl, make you cower in the night. If you knew half of what I've done, you wouldn't be looking at me with those heart eyes. You'd be running away in fear. So run, little rabbit. Run away and leave the big, bad demon alone."

I stared at him. Trying to picture the real demon behind the ridiculous crochet form he was trapped inside. I wondered if he was a deep black like Candy or maybe a crimson marbled orange like Phin. Maybe he was his own unique blend of colors that would make him as beautiful as he was terrifying. I'd ask, but I knew he wouldn't give me an answer. He was so intent on scaring me away, like I was a child who pictured him as a prince charming type. As if I was a princess sitting just waiting to be saved. Ugh. Men were idiots no matter what the species.

"What if I don't care? What if I am perfectly fine with whatever you've done in the past? Do you really think I don't understand you're a demon? That the girls and I haven't thought about what that means for any of us? You're sitting there trying to tell me you're evil, and yet you've treated me better than almost anyone I've had in my life before."

"That's a sad fucking statement on your life."

"I'm aware." We stood there, staring each other down for a long, endless moment.

"Get your ass in bed." He didn't have to tell me twice. I headed toward my bedroom with Jax right behind me. His tentacles wrapped around my waist, stroked up to cup my breasts through my shirt as we walked. "If I were in my body, I'd throw you over my shoulder and carry you to bed. I'd lay your sassy ass over my lap and give you a spanking. I can't do everything I want, but if you want me to fuck you, I'm going to do it my way this time."

He stepped away when we reached my bedroom. I sat on the edge of the bed, uncertain what was going to come next. Trembling in anticipation. I wanted whatever he was going to give me.

I wanted it all.

"Get your toy, sweetness."

I bit my lower lip and chewed on it, debating.

"I said, get your toy."

Decision made, I slid off of the bed onto the floor and pulled the small chest out from under it. It took only a moment to put in the combination and undo the latches. I opened the lid and waited.

Chapter Seven

"Why Fern, you're just full of surprises, aren't you?" Tentacles sifted through the items in the chest. Most of the contents hidden away in their individual pouches and bags, but it was fairly obvious what the chest was for. "Have you used all of these?"

"No." I watched him grab a large satin bag and pull out a dark green dildo with a suction cup base. It was about eight inches long and wide enough my fist just barely wrapped the entire way around it. "Violet introduced me to a book subscription service. Every month you got a box with a new romance novel and a toy. Some of it doesn't make sense to use alone. Others..."

"Others what, sweetness?"

"They intimidate the hell out of me." Jax put the dildo on the bed and picked up a small, black velvet pouch. My inner muscles clenched at the sight of it. I knew what was in that pouch.

"And this?" He held up the small glass plug

with a pink diamond on the wide flared base. "Have you used this?"

I nodded, unable to admit it out loud. It wasn't something I used often, but it was one of my favorite toys. Which is why it was on top.

"Interesting." He kept shifting through the bags and pouches, peeking inside them at random. "Get undressed and get on the bed."

This time, obedience was easy. Because it was exactly what I wanted. I yanked my sweater over my head, leaving my breasts bare to the air before wiggling my way out of my pants. I started to get onto the bed, but a firm tentacle around my wrist stopped me.

"When I say 'get undressed' I mean everything." He looked down and then back up into my eyes.

My hands trembled as I took my underwear off and dropped them with the rest of my clothes. Completely bare with someone else for the first time, I slid up onto the bed and back until I could rest against the headboard.

A black satin strip appeared in front of me. "I won't do anything you don't like but I want you to trust me. Put this on."

I took the blindfold and stared at it for a long minute. Was I brave enough to do this? Did I trust him? He was a demon.

He was also the person who had been nicer to me than anyone else in my life. Jax had given me no reason to not trust him. He had only ever respected my boundaries and comforted me.

Slowly, I raised the fabric to my eyes and tied it around my head.

"That's my good girl." Tentacles guided me down to lay on my back, my head resting on a pillow. There was a bit of a chill in the air, and goosebumps covered my body.

"Relax." Tentacles smoothed over my skin, leaving waves of heat behind them. God, Jax was always so warm. I could just wrap myself up in him forever.

Nope, not thinking like that. That was the dream of a naive, little girl who was going to get her heart broken. I knew better. I wouldn't let myself hurt my own feelings by building up some fantasy in my head where he was mine.

Jax wasn't my happily ever after. That wasn't what this was, and I needed to remember that.

Tentacles wrapped around my sides and smoothed up to graze against my chest. My nipples were already hard from the cold, and so sensitive.

"I hate that I'm stuck in this body." Jax said, tracing across my breasts, circling wide, then inward to brush against my nipples. A tease of sensation. "I would give just about anything to taste you."

I shivered, trying to imagine what it would be like to have his mouth on me.

"I'd tease you here." A brush against my right nipple. "And here." A flick against my left nipple. "And I'd spend hours feasting on you here." He trailed along my seam.

The touch was a brush, a tease. It wasn't nearly enough. I couldn't help myself from arching up to get more pressure.

"Needy little thing, aren't you?" Jax pulled away entirely, and I couldn't stop the whine. My nipples were so sensitive and I was already damp and ready. It wouldn't take much to make me come. And I wanted it. I wanted that orgasm.

"Will you stop teasing me?" I begged him, reaching up to push at the blindfold. Tentacles wrapped around my wrists.

"Uh-uh-uh. None of that now." He brought my hands down to my sides and pressed down. "Keep them here. There's a good girl."

"Jax, touch me."

"I'm going to. Patience, sweetness. I'll give you what you need. Just be patient." A vibrator whirred to life, and I tensed, waiting to feel it on my body. But after a moment, it turned off, and the room went silent again.

I jerked when a tentacle wrapped around my right leg. "Shhh, gentle sweetness. It's just me. I promised I won't do anything you don't like."

He pressed my knee up to my chest, leaving me very exposed. Another tentacle took my wrist and guided it to my knee. "Hold this here. Try to relax."

I knew what was coming, but I still jerked as cool liquid landed on my ass and trailed down to my rear entrance. The plug was unexpectedly warm when Jax trailed it along the same path as the lube before settling firmly against my hole. I tried to relax as he pressed the glass plug against me, but I knew I was too tense for it to work.

After years of purity rings and abstinence only education, I had finally come to a good, healthy place with my sexuality. I was comfortable in my body and in finding my own pleasure. I could ignore most of the bullshit I'd had dumped into my head since childhood and enjoy my body.

Apparently, the comfort I'd learned in my self-exploration did not translate to being comfortable with another person. Laying there with my knee to my chest and my ass exposed to Jax, I had never been more tense in my life.

I also hated Jax a little bit, for being right about finding pleasure alone being different than finding it with someone else. I could never tell him. His ego would become too big for either of us to bear.

"It's okay sweetness. We'll take it nice and slow." He put a little more pressure against it before easing off. "Oh, the things I could do to you in my true form. I'd make you ride my cock and when you've taken as much of me as you can, I'd fill this tight little hole right here," he pressed the plug in deeper and I flinched at the stretch. He pulled back a little before doing it again, deeper.

"I'd stuff you so full with my cock and my tail you'd forget where I start and you end."

I jerked up, dropping my leg. I gasped and whined as the unexpected movement forced the plug home. It wasn't particularly large, but it was big enough to stretch and make me hyper aware of it. It was a deliciously sinful feeling once I adjusted to it.

"I told you to stay put, sweetness."

"Did you just say you have a tail? And that you want to fuck me with it?" I reached for the blindfold, wanting to see him for this conversation. A tail? Really?

"Hand down, Fern." He circled my wrists and pinned them to my sides. "Yes, I have a tail. It's very sensitive and hell, it would feel so good to have you squeezing it with that impossibly tight little hole."

I flushed hot, trying to imagine it. But, a tail? Phin and Candy don't have tails." I'd seen them both in full demon form. Candy didn't look much different from a human, if you could get past the jet-black skin, purple lips, and glowing blue eyes. Phin was the same, very much a normal man. You know, if normal was built like a Greek god with red skin and black lips, nails, and eyes. Oh, and large ram's horns curling out from his forehead. But a tail?

"Sweetness, you're currently fucking a demon sent by a lord of Hell. I'm a walking, talking toy. And a tail is what's tripping you up?"

"Yes, okay." I sighed and flopped backward. "Do you have cloven feet too? A donkey's behind? Anything else I should know?"

"A great many things you should know, I'm sure." He released my hands and gently spread my knees out. A quick buzzing sound was all the warning I got before the vibrator pressed against my exposed clit.

"Now, do you want to discuss my appearance, or do you want me to make you come?"

"Yes, that one. Please!" I thrust up, trying to get more pressure from the vibrator, but Jax pulled it back, teasing me.

Tentacles wrapped around my ankles and thighs, pulling my legs further apart. The air felt cold in comparison to Jax's heat and goosebumps covered the upper half of my body. My already hard nipples tightened to the point of pain. My pussy clenched, causing me to squeeze around the plug. The variety of different temperatures and sensations overwhelmed me, sending me right to the edge.

"Damn, I love how sensitive you are," Jax said. He moved the vibrator down to circle my opening, gathering the moisture there. My inner muscles spasmed and my clit throbbed, both desperate for more.

"So needy. All this time, I thought you were this sweet, innocent, little virgin. But you're not, are you? You're a greedy slut just begging for someone to fill this pretty hole."

The vibrator disappeared and I couldn't bite back my whine. It was replaced with a soft, hot tentacle. He brushed my spread lips, his touch the barest of teases over my clit. Sliding the limb down, he circled my opening, collecting the wetness I could feel gathered there.

"Look at the mess you're making. You're so

wet for me, sweetness. I just want to drink you up."

Suddenly, he released my legs entirely, and I felt his body press against my pussy. For a brief moment I worried about the mess, but then he rocked himself against my clit and I no longer cared. My hands went to the ball that made up his main mass and I pressed down, moving against him. It wasn't enough. I needed more friction.

I rolled over, straddling his body. My ass clenched around the plug as I brought my knees under me for better leverage as I began to grind against him. He'd gone soft beneath me, no longer feeling like a yarn-covered basketball. He was just firm enough to stimulate my clit as I moved against him.

Two tentacles grabbed my arms and tugged backward, forcing my torso up, thrusting my breasts out. Another set came up to toy with them, weighing the globes, teasing my nipples. I was already a whining, moaning mess. And that was before he gripped my hips and helped me move faster, harder.

"Oh my god," I moaned, as I neared my peak. Jax said something. I could feel the vibration between my legs and hear the muffled sound, but I was too wrapped up in sensation to turn the muffled sounds into words.

He muttered or groaned; I couldn't tell but the slight vibration of the sound was enough to send me over the edge. My body went impossibly tight before climax swept over me. I cried out as my inner walls clenched around nothing. A tentacle shoved its way into my mouth and I bit down, trying to muffle the sounds as I felt liquid gather and pool at my entrance.

My movements were frantic and Jax's grip on my hips kept me moving against him until I was so over-sensitized, I was nearly in tears. I slumped limply forward, dangling in the tentacles' grasp. Finally, Jax stopped forcing my movements and released me. I fell face-first onto the bed. I was too languid and exhausted to catch myself. The tentacle in my mouth pulled out and pressed against my body as he slowly, agonizingly, brought it out from underneath me.

He tapped my hip and butt gently. Taking it as a sign that he wanted me to move, I shifted and lifted my hips higher to give him wiggle room. My body was too spent to even roll onto my side.

"I'm pretty sure if I were mortal, you would have killed me just then." Soft, damp material nuzzled the curve of my butt where it met my leg. "My gods, you're exquisite."

I flushed. I was equal parts preening under his praise and embarrassed by how wet he felt against my skin. I had practically drenched him in my come.

"How are you feeling sweetness?" I offered him a limp thumbs up, which caused him to laugh. He reached up and removed my blindfold. I blinked against the sudden light, slamming my hand to my eyes with a groan. It was followed by another, as I finally stretched out my legs and flopped onto my stomach. Tentacles covered every part of me, bringing heat and massaging my muscles.

"I'm going to need your words," Jax pushed. "Are you okay?"

"'S'all good," I slurred. "So sleepy."

Jax chuckled. The dark sound made my pussy clench.

"Oh Fern, I'm not nearly done with you."

Chapter Eight

"No more." I begged, even as I shifted along with Jax's directions to spread my legs. When I wasn't fast enough for him, he slapped the plug in my ass. I yelped.

"You can take it." He pinned my legs in place. He moved his body to rest between my splayed thighs. "So fucking pretty."

Heat suffused me, knowing he was staring straight at my swollen, spread, and soaking wet pussy. Even after everything we'd done, it still felt taboo and embarrassing.

"How I'd love to see this pretty little cunt spread wide by my cock." A gentle brush with a tentacle. And then there was a firm push by something solid and cold. I shifted and twisted until I could look over my shoulder. Yep, he was holding the green dildo. I wasn't positive I could take it.

Before I could caution him, Jax pushed the toy deeper and deeper, sliding in with little resistance after my orgasm. I was so damn wet, it went smoothly. There was still a stretch but it wasn't as bad as I had expected it to be.

"Good girl. You're taking that cock so well." I clenched as the praise set me aflame. "You might just be able to take me, sweetness. This little toy doesn't measure up, but your cunt is just begging for more."

I whimpered as he bottomed the toy out against my cervix. I was so full already; I couldn't imagine taking more. Briefly, I wondered if it mattered. It was very unlikely I'd ever sleep with him in his true form.

The only way Candy and Phin had escaped their yarny forms was when my friends fell well and truly in love with them and they loved my friends in return. That wasn't what was happening here. Jax was humoring me. Doing me a favor by indulging my bucket list item of having sex before I died. There was no chance he was falling in love with someone like me.

Jax slowly dragged the dildo out of me and quickly pushed it deep again. My thoughts ripped back to the moment. I cried out and immediately gagged on a tentacle. I choked as it went too deep and hit my gag reflex.

"Shh, you don't want the neighbors to hear what a naughty girl you are, do you?"

I whined and shook my head around his limb.

"There's a good girl. Now keep quiet while I

fuck you with this dildo and imagine it's my cock buried all the way inside of you."

Jax continued the slow pull out, dragging the ribbed shaft and flared head over every pleasure point. The single deep thrust pushed the head of the fake cock against my sensitive cervix in just the way I liked. It felt like forever and no time at all before I was a writhing, whining mess, reduced to using my body to beg for the orgasm I so desperately needed.

"Does my needy girl need to come?" Jax teased.

I nodded rapidly, trying to use my arms to push my body back harder against the toy. It was useless. The bottom half of my body was so firmly pinned I couldn't get the pounding or friction I needed.

"Okay sweetness, I'm going to let you come on the count of five. Five."

I wiggled in his grasp and tried to use my arms for better leverage, absolutely desperate.

"Four." His movements sped up. The slow drag was now a rapid jack-hammering in and out.

"Three." A tentacle moved between my legs and began toying with my clit. I knew right away it would leave me over sensitized and sore, but in that moment, I didn't care.

"Two." He released my legs. I shoved myself up on all fours and thrusted my hips back against the toy as he moved it.

"One." My entire body was a tense bow, just waiting to break. Pleasure was almost painful as it pooled in my belly. Our movements were frantic and sloppy. There was no smooth slide or fitness, just the primal need to come.

"Now, Fern. Come for me."

There was a sharp slap on the base of the plug. And another. I screamed into the tentacle gag as I came. The pressure in my stomach moved to my pussy, setting it spasming. I was so wet I could hear the toy squelch as it pounded into me.

I closed my eyes and pretended, just for a moment, that it was Jax fucking into me. That it was his cock driving me over the edge instead of the poor silicone substitute.

And then I just let myself fall.

Chapter Nine

"Fern, you need to wake up." Soft touches brushed my tangled hair out of my face. I moaned, but turned my head to look at Jax.

He was soaked. His entire body and limbs were dark with wetness. I could feel myself turn red.

"Oh sweetness, I love how easily you blush. This isn't all you. I cleaned up. I also brought you some water. You need to hydrate."

I groaned, but somehow found the energy to turn over and prop myself up on my pillows. Jax handed me the water before bringing the blanket at the foot of my bed up. He tucked me in as I drained the glass.

"Thank you." I handed him back the glass and tugged the blankets tighter around me. My eyes were already beginning to droop again.

"That's it, sweetness." A damp tentacle brushed my hair back from my face and kept soothing it into place. "Get some rest. You need it."

I snuggled deeper into the pillows and let his deep voice and soft pets send me back to sleep.

The next morning, I woke to a wonderful mix of languid and sore. It was like the day after a really great workout. Which I supposed was accurate enough.

I took extra time in the shower, letting the hot water pummel my aching muscles. Memories of the things I did had me flushed and wishing I didn't have to get to work so soon. I wanted Jax again. Now that I knew how good sex with a partner could be, I wanted to experience it again. It was so much more satisfying and addicting with someone else.

Was it like that with everyone? Or was it just because it was Jax? I knew the extra limbs added to the experience, but even without those, would we be as good with anyone else?

"Don't go there, Fern." I warned myself as I braided my damp hair and did my makeup. "Don't romanticize him. He isn't your forever."

I pulled on a long-sleeve maxi dress and called it good. I was running late after my marathon shower, and I still needed to grab a cup of coffee and see Jax before I left.

His voice floated out of the kitchen as I walked down the hall in my stocking feet.

"What do you expect me to do?" His voice was growly and frustrated. "What is something like me supposed to do with someone like her? I just settle down and enjoy small town living for the next century? Be real."

I stepped back, slapping a hand over my mouth to muffle the sob that choked me. Spinning around, I headed the opposite direction and out the door. There was no way I could face him.

I knew, of course I knew. I wasn't stupid. But knowing someone would never want you and hearing it were very different things. Especially when your dumb, stupid heart failed to pay attention to your head and went and fell in love with the demon who couldn't bear the thought of a life with you.

It took a lot of effort to hold it together, more than the stupid demon deserved. I waited in my car until just before the bell so I could avoid Violet. She would have given me sympathy and offered violence on my behalf, and I couldn't handle either right then.

Our lunches and planning periods were at different times, so I managed to avoid her all day. Until the mandatory staff meeting after school. She cornered me as soon as it was over and dragged me to her classroom.

"Spill." She demanded as she stood in front of the door with her arms crossed. She was shorter than me but she was an immovable force. So, I did the only thing I could. I dropped down into her chair and spilled.

"I'm an idiot and I'm going to end up in Hell. Which can't be more miserable than living with a broken heart."

"Broken, who? Oh no, not you too!" She rubbed her hands over her face.

I buried my face in my hands and let the tears come. The stupid tears from my stupid heart that refused to listen to me.

"You don't understand, Vi. But it doesn't matter. Jax doesn't want me."

"Are you sure? Really sure?"

"Positive. He's not interested in anything with me. I was a pity fuck, and I knew better." Violet handed me a tissue and wrapped her arms around me. I rested my head against her stomach, taking in her affection.

"I'm sorry, sweetie. It's probably for the best. They're demons. I don't care how devoted they seem, there has to be a catch."

I nodded. But a scary voice inside my head asked if I would care about the consequences if I got to be with Jax. It whispered anything might be worth it.

Chapter Ten

I t was Tuesday night before I went back to the apartment. Violet had dragged me home with her the night before and plied me with pasta and wine. We talked about the new lead she found about a possible way out of our deal.

I didn't hold much hope, but I listened to her explain the path she took to finding the origins of the spell book we'd used to do the original "spell" that bound us into the deal in the first place.

She offered to let me stay with her, or come with me to face Jax, but I turned her down. I couldn't avoid my apartment forever. And Violet was very much a "fight now, talk later" personality. She would only add kerosene to an already miserable situation.

The phone rang as I pulled into the parking lot but I hit the ignore button. My phone was filled with dozens of missed calls and texts from Jax. I'd been ignoring him all day but I wanted to handle him face to face.

Actually, I didn't want to handle him at all. But I was a goddamn grown-up who had spent thousands of dollars on therapy to learn how to demand my needs be met. And right then, I needed Jax gone.

I was trying to fit my key into the lock when the door flew open. I stumbled back a step, turning a glare on Jax.

"About fucking time!" Jax growled.

But it wasn't Jax. The creature before me wasn't a purple and blue ball of yarn standing eye-level with me on eight tentacles.

No, this being towered over me. His skin was deep purple, his eyes were endless black pools glaring at me. He had horns that curved up from his brow, standing nearly a foot tall. He was both terrifying and beautiful.

Clawed hands grabbed my arms and hauled me inside. He slammed the door shut and shoved me back against it.

"What the hell have you done, Fern?" The beast demanded.

I shook my head. I didn't understand. The hulking mass was Jax. It was his voice, his touch. I just didn't understand why he was here. How he was here in his demon form.

"You sneaked out of the apartment yesterday morning without a word, leaving me worried about you all day. The next thing I know I'm back in my rooms looking like this. I need you to tell me what you did."

"I did nothing!" I yell at him, wrenching out

of his grasp and stomping into the apartment. "Looks like your part is done. You're free to leave."

I knew what happened. Oh, I knew. The deal was I had to find my love. Nothing in the contract said he had to love me back. My stupid, traitorous heart had fallen and now I got to have it stomped all over.

"You know damn well I can't do that." Jax growled, following me. He grabbed my hand and spun me around. I stumbled into his chest. He pinned my hand behind my back, keeping me pressed against him.

"How did you get out of the deal?" He growled. The sound resonated in my chest and made my heart race.

"I didn't, you big idiot." I used my free hand to push against him, but he didn't budge. "Let me go!"

"Fern," He growled, baring his fangs. It was a demand, a warning.

"Jax, just go. You have your life back and it looks like I have mine. We don't have to make this into something that it isn't."

"And what is this, Fern? Because the way I see it, if you didn't break the deal, you must have fulfilled the terms." He brushed my hair back over my shoulder before fisting his hand in it. "And I know damned well that I'm the only male you've been around."

He tugged my hair to force my head back so I

was looking up at him. Those black eyes bore into me.

"Yes, okay! I, like a fucking idiot, fell in love with you. Look at me, begging for love in all the wrong places again."

The words were barely out before Jax's mouth crashed down on mine.

Chapter Eleven

His kiss was brutal and consuming. He used the grip on my hair to angle my head where he wanted it. His tongue demanded access to my mouth. It was longer than a normal tongue and twined around mine.

The hand holding my arm behind my back released me to slide down to my ass. The other in my hair followed to lift me up off the ground and against him. My hands went around his neck to hold on, my legs wrapped around his waist.

I was an average height, but he was probably seven feet tall before the horns which left me wrapped around his stomach. I could feel the ridges of his muscles move under me as he panted. It was a sinful tease.

"Tell me, sweetness." He growled against my mouth. "I need to hear you say it again."

He scraped his teeth along my neck before nipping at the spot where my neck met my shoul-der. I whimpered, my brain going fuzzy.

"Huh? What?"

"Damn it, Fern." He kissed and nuzzled his way back up my neck. "I've been obsessed with you since about five minutes after I got here. Sweet, innocent little Fern who looks like an angel but has the mind of a devil."

I flushed, heat running through my entire body. I couldn't process what he was saying. He wanted me?

"But you said you weren't going to touch me." I dug my hands into the long black hair flowing down to mid-back. I fisted it, trying to ground myself.

"And how long did that last?" Sharp teeth bit into my neck just below my ear. Not hard enough to break the skin, but enough to make me jerk in his arms. "I was too weak to resist you. As hard as I tried, I couldn't keep my hands off of you."

His hands tightened on my ass and he rubbed me against his abs, made me moan. I was so turned on that alone was almost enough to make me come. But I need to understand.

"Why? Why would you want to keep your hands off of me when I was literally begging for it? Do you know how hard that was for me?" I yanked his hair, forcing him to look at me. "Are you going to decide I'm not good enough for you and leave like everyone else does? I don't want this if you don't mean it."

"Not good enough for me?" He growled. Jax shifted me so I was balancing on just one of his hands so he could cup my face in the other.

"Sweetness, I'm not good enough for you. You're all things sweet and light. I should let you go right now before I have time to drag you down into Hell with me."

"Don't you dare." dug my nails into his shoulders, daring him to let go of me. "Don't you fucking dare."

"You need to understand something, Fern." His hand moved back into my hair where he fisted it. "If I touch you, really touch you, then there's no going back. You're going to be mine. I need you to understand what that means.

"I'm a sex demon. I know ways to make you come that even your dirty little mind cannot imagine. I could take you over and over again until I drain the life right out of you. I'm not the nice guy. I'm not the one that's going to give you the fairy tale ending. I'm the one who is going to fuck you until you're hoarse and then do it again."

I moaned, writhing against him. He was trying to scare me off but he didn't understand. That level of want was just what I needed.

"Who said I wanted the fairy tale ending? I just want you." I brought his mouth to me and kissed him. Digging my nails into the back of his neck I held him in place so I could thrust my tongue into his mouth to battle with his. My hips ground against him, seeking more friction. I was frantic for his touch and I needed him. Needed him to touch me, to fuck me, to love me.

He released my hair and slid me down his body, pausing to grind me against the hard length of him in his pants. I reached out to touch it, but he grabbed my wrist.

"Not yet, sweetness." He set my feet on the floor and backed me into the wall. "I'm going to get my fill of you first."

Jax dropped onto his knees before me, slowly bringing my skirt up over my hips. He grabbed one of my hands and forced the bunched material into it.

"Have I ever told you how much I love that you're always in dresses? The number of times I fantasized about just this?"

He leaned forward and nuzzled his face between my legs. It was reminiscent of how he'd nuzzled me before.

"I nearly drowned in you before, but everything in that form was muted." He licked a hot swipe over me, through my underwear and I arched against the wall. "I can't wait to get the taste of you on my tongue."

He licked again, the muted sensation was a tease and had me panting. Before I could demand more, he slid my underwear down my legs and tossed them to the side.

"Hold on, sweetness."

That was the only warning I got before he lifted one of my legs over his shoulder and dove in. His tongue was impossibly hot as he licked over me. He licked long swipes up from my entrance to my clit, pausing to flick it before doing it again and again. It was good. So good. But it wasn't enough.

I moved against him, both hands fisting my skirt to try to watch him as he devoured me. Without warning, he sucked my clit into his mouth and I cried out. My legs started to shake, and I grabbed onto one of his horns for balance.

Jax groaned, and the sound echoed through me. Pleasure gathered low, and I felt myself getting wet.

"That's it, love. Play with my horns. They're so sensitive for you." He sucked my clit back into his mouth, flicking it with his tongue, and I had no choice but to squeeze down on his horn. It was the only thing keeping me standing at that point. I was close to orgasm when he stopped sucking and moved to drive his long tongue into me, fucking me with it.

I slid my hand down to the base of his horn and he groaned again. His horns were hard and smooth under my hand as I stroked him. He growled and groaned against me. His tongue pulled out to lap at my clit. It was my turn to moan when he drove a finger inside me. I froze for a moment, remembering the claws.

"Don't worry, sweetness. I won't do anything to hurt you." Jax stared up at me from under my dress. His face damp, and those black eyes somehow spoke volumes. I nodded, trusting him.

He let loose a low growl and returned to licking and sucking at my clit. One finger became two and then three. The stretch was almost unbearable. But then he curled those fingers and rubbed at that sensitive spot that sent my head reeling.

I dropped my skirt and grabbed both of his horns, shamelessly dragging his face closer. His free hand came up to my stomach and pinned me in place just as he latched onto my clit and sucked.

Pleasure flooded me as I came on Jax's face. My legs gave out. I remained upright only by the hand on my stomach and the grip I had on his horns. I was chanting his name as he continued to lick and suck and stroke me through the orgasm.

Slowly, Jax pulled his hand free from me and brushed my skirt off of his face. He reached up to press his fingers to my lips. I flicked my tongue out to lick them. I'd never tasted myself before, but the musky mix of my come and the saltiness of his skin wasn't what I expected.

I noticed his claws had receded into normal-ish, if pointed and black could be called normal, fingernails. I flicked my tongue out over them and Jax groaned.

"You taste so fucking sweet, just as I knew you would. But I've to fuck you. I'm going to go insane if I don't get inside of you soon."

Chapter Twelve

Jax surged to his feet, carrying me wrapped around him again.

"Are you ready for that?"

I nodded quickly, and Jax laughed as he carried us into the bedroom. His mouth never left me, kissing my mouth, my neck, the tops of my breasts. I was one big erogenous zone. Everywhere he touched and kissed and sucked set my body to flames.

He set me down beside the bed and grabbed the crew neck of the dress I was wearing. In one smooth slice of his hands, the dress was in two.

"Hey! That was Violet's." I protested as he shoved the shredded pieces off me. When he reached for the front of my bra with those claws, I put my hand up and shoved back. "Don't you dare. Do you have any idea how hard it is to find a bra that fits?"

"Then you'd better take it off fast. I'm losing my mind over here." He yanked his black t-shirt over his head and I froze. I'd felt his abs against my body when I'd been wrapped in his arms, but seeing was a different story. He was absolutely ripped. Every inch of him was perfect and defined, and my mouth watered at the idea of tasting him.

"I like the sin in your eyes, love. But if you don't get naked in the next two seconds, I will destroy those pretty underwear and not feel bad about it for a second."

Unclasping my bra with fumbling hands, I tossed it aside and reached to shove my underwear down and off. It was my favorite set and there was no way I was letting him destroy it.

Jax had unbuttoned his dark pants but froze to stare at me. He reached out and traced an areola with a sharp nail before cupping my breasts in his hands. His thumbs came up to strum at my nipples as he stared down at me.

"You are utter perfection."

"I'm not." The words were out before I could think to stop them. I knew I wasn't perfect. I was riddled with flaws.

Jax dropped my breasts to cup my face. "You are perfect. Every inch, every thought, every flaw you think you have is perfect. Because those are the things that make you who you are and who you are is perfect for me. You're mine and I plan on worshiping you like you deserve."

I blinked back tears. That was hands down the nicest thing anyone had ever said about me, and I swear my heart swelled in my chest like a cartoon character. I reached up to grab his neck and drag him down to me to kiss.

"I love you," I said against his lips. He froze before dragging me closer and devouring me.

As hot as I was burning before, it had nothing on the inferno blazing through us now. I reached down to unzip Jax's pants and shove them down his hips. When his penis bumped against my bare stomach, I froze.

I had thought he was exaggerating about being bigger than the green dildo, but the monster between his legs was definitely bigger. I stopped shoving his pants down and stared at him.

"You're killing me, sweetness." Jax groaned, grabbing my hand and bringing it to him. I wrapped my hand around him and my fingers couldn't touch.

He was thick and long. The head was such a dark purple it looked like a bad bruise and I briefly wondered if it hurt. I slid my hand down him and gasped at the feel of bumps all down his shaft.

When I looked up, he just grinned. I stroked him again, curious about the feel. It was definitely not like any penis I'd touched before. I mean, I didn't have a lot to compare to, but I'd remember a bumpy penis.

"Jax?" It was so big, so hard. There was just no way.

"Don't worry, love. It'll fit. That sweet little pussy was made for me." He gently pried my hand off of him and shoved his pants the rest of the way off. He backed me toward the bed before scooping me up and laying me in the middle.

He climbed over me and bent to take a nipple in his hot mouth. Not normal hot, but nearly burning hot. It was so intense I cried out. He froze and looked up at me. I nodded down at him and brought a hand to the back of his head to hold him in place. It was surprising, but it felt so damn good.

He switched to the other nipple. As he sucked and licked at it, he brought a hand up my leg and dragged it up to drape over his hip. He continued down until his fingers were teasing at my opening. I was still wet and sensitive from the first orgasm and bucked against him.

"You're so damn sensitive." He murmured, against my boob. "I can't get enough of how you react to me."

"You've had how much practice? Maybe I'm not sensitive and you're just that good."

"Centuries of being a parasite on other's pleasure and I've never had anyone react to me like you do. And I've never cared if they did. You're the only one I want to touch. You're the only one I need." He bent his head to take my lips again.

After a blistering kiss, he punched up onto his haunches and spread my knees wide, giving him full access to my body. He brought his thumb to my clit and drew slow circles that slowly had me out of my mind.

"One more, sweetness. Give me one more so you're nice and relaxed and then I'll give you my cock." He slid two fingers inside of me while he maintained that steady pace with his thumb and I couldn't do anything but moan, and nod.

I was already sensitive and primed, so this orgasm came quick and hard, leaving me panting and clenching around his fingers.

Before I'd come down, he was back over me, mouth on mine.

The head of his cock rested against my opening, and I squirmed beneath him.

"Are you sure you're ready for this?" He asked, holding himself above me. "We don't have to do anything you don't want."

I hitched my legs up to wrap around him, pulling his hips down toward mine. I grabbed his upper arms and nodded.

"Don't you dare stop now." I demanded, digging my nails into his arms and my heels into his back. He chuckled and kissed me as he pushed forward with his hips. I clenched around him and whimpered. I stretched so wide it was nearly painful.

Jax slid back until just his head was inside of me and paused for me to catch my breath before sliding in again. Even after my orgasm, I was too tight for him.

"Hold on." He kissed me.

I grabbed him around the shoulders, not letting him go.

He chuckled. "I'm just going to get something. I won't even leave the room."

Slowly, I unwrapped my arms and legs from

him. He got up and reached under my bed for the chest of toys. We had left it unlocked, so Jax could open the lid. I was afraid he had given up on having sex with me until he produced a bottle of lube and rejoined me on the bed.

"I'm big sweetness. I don't want to hurt you." He dribbled some of the liquid on the head of his cock and used his hand to coat the length of him. He bent back over me and lined himself up with my opening.

This time, he could press a little deeper. I gasped as the bumps on his shaft dragged against my walls. They touched every part of me as he dragged himself back out and thrust in again, going even deeper.

He continued that slow pace for what seemed like forever. I couldn't stop squirming under him as he stimulated every part of me. Finally, finally, he pushed deep one more time, and I felt him press against my cervix. I didn't think he was all the way in but there was nowhere else to go.

Jax didn't seem to mind that I couldn't take all of him as he groaned and leaned down to take my mouth. He ground his hips down and every part of me lit up with sensation.

"Fuck, you're so tight. You're taking me so well." He slid almost entirely out and then back again. I cried out at the sensation. "Do I need to get a gag, sweetness? Or can you be quiet for me?"

I slapped a hand to my mouth and nodded. I

would never be able to face the neighbors if they heard me screaming through the walls.

"First chance I get, we're getting a nice house out in the woods. I want to hear you screaming my name as I fuck this sweet pussy." He began to move, steady strokes that had me panting behind my hand.

He slid a hand between us and circled my clit. It only took a few brushes of his fingers before I exploded.

My pussy clenched around him so hard it nearly hurt. My back bowed, and I had to bite the side of my hand to keep me from making too much noise as Jax fucked me through it.

"Fuck, fuck, fuck. You're going to destroy me." Jax pumped faster and then went tight as I spasmed around him. I could feel his penis throbbing inside of me as he finished.

Chapter Thirteen

Cold washed through me. We hadn't talked about birth control. I couldn't believe I was so stupid. Just like my mother.

"Hey, hey Fern. Come back to me." Jax brushed a hand through my hair. His face was drawn.

I shoved against him. Needing him out of me. He must have seen something on my face because he pulled out, causing me to spasm again. But I couldn't enjoy the pleasure as panic swirled through my brain.

Sure, I wasn't likely to run off on my child like my mother, but what if I wasn't able to love a baby like I should? What if in the end I was no better than Grandmother, cold and distant?

"What's wrong? Talk to me." Jax sounded worried as I climbed out of bed on shaky legs, almost losing my balance as I crossed the room. I needed to get to the bathroom. I needed to clean up. I needed to think.

I could feel Jax's come sliding out of me and down my leg, and the sensation sent a shiver down my spine.

Before I could leave the room, Jax was in front of me, holding my arms, bending to be at my level.

"Talk to me, love. What happened? Did I hurt you? Was that too fast? Too soon?" His distress was clear and nearly matched mine. As much as I was panicking, I couldn't leave him out here thinking it was his fault. I should have said something. We should have talked.

"We didn't use a condom." I said, begging him to understand.

"Oh Fern," He kissed my forehead, stroking his hands down my arms. "You're safe. Demons don't get diseases. I would never do anything to put you at risk like that."

"I didn't, I wasn't..." I pushed my hands through my messy hair and dropped them. "I don't want kids."

Jax stared at me for a long moment. I was just about to shove past him and run out of the room when he scooped me up in his arms and carried me back to the bed. He sat on the side with me on his lap. His arms wrapped around me tight enough that I knew I wasn't going anywhere.

"There is no such thing as a demon-human hybrid. From the moment I became a demon, my chances at children were gone. I never even thought about it." He brushed his hand through my hair and over my back, soothing me. "I'm sorry I made you panic. It just isn't something I've had to consider in a very long time. I never even asked how you felt about kids."

I buried my face in his chest, relief washing over me. I wasn't going to be like my mother making a heat of the moment decision, ruining someone else's life. It would be okay. I trusted Jax not to lie to me.

"But Fern," Jax used a finger to tilt my face up at him. "I know what you're thinking. You're nothing like your grandmother. You'd make a wonderful mother."

"It doesn't matter. I wouldn't want to risk it." I wrapped my arms tight around his waist and settled into the warmth of him.

"If you ever change your mind, we could do it. Not us, but there are lots of children out there who need a mom as amazing as you. I don't want you to miss out on anything in life because you chose me."

I laughed, imagining Jax in full demon form picking up a child from school. I knew he wouldn't. Demons could take human form and maintain it indefinitely. But I liked Jax's demon form. He made me warm and feel safe.

"Maybe." I said, knowing I wouldn't change my mind. I was perfectly okay being fun aunt Fern to Jasmine's kids. I had my students. That was enough for me.

"I just want you to be happy. Whatever you

want, I want to give it to you." Jax pressed his lips to my temple. I settled into him. Wrapping my arms around his biceps, I settled my head against his broad chest and let myself be soothed.

Epilogue

"I can't believe I ran into another dead end. I swear this curse didn't exist before we found it." Violet downed the rest of her beer and set the bottle on the ground by her feet. "It just doesn't make any sense. Honestly, nothing makes sense anymore."

"I'm sure you'll figure it out." I offered, along with another bottle. She took the beer but sneered at my empty platitude. We all knew it was empty. Violet was the last of us unmated and had the most riding on finding a way out of the contract.

Jax wrapped his arms around me and pulled me down into his lap. I settled into him, loving how warm he was. Even in his human form he kept his demonic heat. While his human form was nice to look at – the epitome of tall, dark and handsome – I always missed his true demon form when he was in human skin.

It was probably too early in the year for a bonfire, but no one had tried to talk me down when I suggested it. It was possible they were too tired to argue with me and just wanted the beer and pizza I promised them.

Today was officially the first day in our new house. Jax, as promised, had found a place without any neighbors for miles. It was an older farmhouse, which meant we needed to sand the floors, update the bathroom and kitchen, and I demanded we paint the walls. After years of living with Grandmother, who decided how things should look and then apartments, I wanted to do everything to make this house my home. Our home.

Jax had spoiled me, letting me do anything I wanted to the place to make it exactly what I dreamed of. He refused to tell me how he had the money to buy a house and do all the renovations. And honestly, I wasn't sure I wanted to know. Some questions were probably better left unanswered.

"It's almost May." Violet pointed out. "I have four months left and I'm getting nowhere. I haven't even gotten a pet demon of my own."

Jax growled, a little at being referred to as a pet. I patted his chest gently before twining my fingers with his.

"I take offense to the word pet," Candy told Violet. "It seems rather offensive."

"You're basically a domesticated wild creature that lives and dies for Clover's whims. You're a pet." Clover tossed the lid from her bottle at

Violet, who knocked it off-course with the back of her hand. I was pretty sure she was trying to catch it, but I wasn't going to call her out.

"I wonder why you haven't gotten a pet," Jasmine mused. She hadn't helped me move, since she didn't want to pay for a sitter all day, but she came for the bonfire and to get Phin. She, like me, snuggled on her demon's lap. The stress that used to permanently live on her face was gone and there was a type of calm there I'd never seen before. I love that for her, almost as much as I loved it for me.

"Not a pet," Jax growled. His arms tightened around me, daring me to argue. I pressed a kiss to his cheek and bit my tongue. I'd totally be teasing him with it later.

"Okay, fine," Jasmine said. "But my question remains. Why hasn't Violet gotten a demon? Candy showed up right away, Phin and Jax three months later. It's been eight months and Violet still hasn't seen one. What's up with that?"

The demons looked at each other but said nothing. I felt like they knew more than they were saying, but I wasn't prepared to call Jax out in front of a crowd.

"Demon Lords don't tell us much." Phin's tone was measured, and I was certain there was more going on here. "We pretty much just go where we're told."

"But that doesn't matter, right Violet?" Clover asked. "You have Braden now and he seems pretty great. Longest you've tolerated a man in years." Violet winced, and I shot her a sympathetic look.

Clover never did pull punches and Violet was pretty notorious for her short attention span where men were concerned.

"Three months does not forever make." Violet said with a shrug.

I wished I had an answer for her. I'd tried to pry information out of Jax but he said he didn't know what the plan for Violet was. He only knew he was sent to protect me until the terms of the bargain were met. I worried that he might be taken from me but he promised it was highly unlikely.

Demons like him were a dime a dozen and often spent lifetimes on Earth. He promised me he wasn't going anywhere and I was choosing to believe him.

Trusting that was hard. Until Violet, Clover, and Jasmine I'd never had anyone who wanted to be there for me. But I wanted to trust Jax. I wanted to believe in him. I wanted to believe in us.

Jax may swear he's not the fairy tale ending but I couldn't imagine a better one. He may be a demon but he was the best thing to ever happen to me and I couldn't wait to see what our forever looked like. Even if I did end up in Hell, it would be worth it with Jax at my side.

Bonus Epilogue

"I want a puppy."

"I want you to stop starting conversations with weird declarative statements." Jax said, tossing the words over his shoulder from where he was plating the tacos he'd made us for dinner. He was in full, blue demon form, wearing nothing but a pair of tight leather pants. I sat on the table with my head on my hand, watching the muscles in his back shift and move.

Sometimes, the reality of my life still shocked me. It'd been months since Jax and I had gotten together. Since we'd bought and created our home together. It was nearly the anniversary of casting our spell. So much had changed in the year.

"But random declarative statements work so well for me," I said with a smile as Jax joined me at the large butcher block island and set a plate in front of me.

"You're not getting a puppy." Jax slid onto the

stool next to me and tugged me closer until our legs brushed. I loved that about him. He was fine doing our own things, but he always preferred to be touching me. I was pretty sure the constant contact and reassurance was for my benefit, but he never made it feel like he was humoring my abandonment issues.

I waited until he picked up his taco and took a large bite.

"Fine, then I want a baby." The choke was satisfying. I pounded him helpfully on the back and waited until his coughing was under control before going on.

"I know we can't have one but we could adopt. If a puppy is too much for you, a baby would be great."

Jax glared at me. "You think you're so smart." He wrapped a hand around my throat, holding me firmly as he glared down at me. My pulse rocketed and my nipples tightened to peaks.

"I know I am." I blinked up at him, all innocence.

"Dogs don't like demons." Jax said, running his thumb up the side of my neck to press against my pulse point before sliding back down. "And I know damn well you don't actually want a baby."

I whimpered when he tightened his grip a little. Then jumped when his tail snaked up under my skirt to wrap around my thigh. The tip of it ran along the edge of my panties where my leg met my thigh. I couldn't keep myself from opening my legs for him.

There was no denying I'd become something of a sex addict in the last six months. It had taken me almost thirty years to find someone worth the risk of sex, but now that I'd had it, I couldn't get enough. True, the fact I was with a sex demon who could do things no human man could, probably added to my addiction, but I couldn't deny the fact I was always ready for him.

"Where is this coming from?" The pressure against my throat was firm, and I swallowed against his hand.

"Okay, I don't actually want a baby," I admitted. Jax rewarded me with a brush against the crease of my pussy lips. "But I do want a puppy."

The tip of his tail pulled away, and I bit back a whine. I would not beg.

"I don't know, I just want one. Clover was talking about getting a kitten and Jasmine has the girls and I guess I was just feeling incomplete somehow. I'm allergic to cats and don't want kids, so a puppy seemed like a safe way to shove down the biological clock."

Jax's hand moved up into my hair and he used the grip to angle my head up. He bent down and rested his forehead against mine. His dark eyes bored into mine.

"Am I not enough for you? You can cuddle and pet me whenever you want." His smile was soft and sweet, but I could sense the question beneath it. I wasn't the only one who had abandonment issues.

"Baby, you're everything. If you're so against

it, I'll drop it." I pressed my lips to his and slid my tongue against his lower lip. He opened for me, sucking my tongue deep into his mouth, as his tail came back to brush against my pussy.

"I'm happy the way things are. I love that I get to have you all to myself." I shivered as Jax kissed his way down my neck. His tail pressed hard against my pleasure button.

"Consider it dropped." I wrapped my hand around his horn and directed his head back to mine so I could take his mouth in a kiss. Dinner could wait.

I couldn't.

I undid his pants and slid my hand inside to wrap around his cock. It was already hard for me. My fingers played against the piercings on the underside under his head. They had confused me the first time I saw them, but I'd come to appreciate the smooth, metal rings.

"I need you to fuck me." The words echoed the ones I'd told him months ago. Then it had been a desperate plea to not die a virgin. Now it was a much darker craving. My body was already wet and clenching, begging for his invasion.

"Panties off," he demanded, sliding me off of the stool and to my feet. "Unless you want me to rip them."

"Don't you dare." I yanked my panties off and tossed them aside. I'd pretty much given up on wearing a bra around the house. My demon was impatient and liked the easy access to my body, and I was usually more than happy to accommodate him.

He yanked down my thin dress straps, baring my breasts to his greedy, grasping hands. I gasped when he pinched the nipples just the right side of painful. Then moaned when he spun me around and pushed me to bend over the island. The butcher block was cold under my sensitive peaks, the air conditioning sending a soft chill across my heated flesh.

Jax flipped my skirt up, baring me to him, and I groaned when he didn't hesitate. Technically, he was too big to go in hard and fast without foreplay. But sometimes, the stretch and burn of taking him slow without a lot of preparation was better than all of the lead up in the world.

He entered me in short, slow thrusts. Moving just a little bit deeper with every measured slide of his body into mine. He had one hand between my shoulder blades, keeping me pinned to the island, while the other one was beneath me, pressing and circling my clit as he moved inside of me.

"That's right, love." Jax moved his hand up to grip my hair, forcing me to arch up. "Take my cock, like the good, greedy girl you are."

"Yes," I moaned. I shifted to my elbows so I could cup and pinch at my own breasts. I rolled my nipples as Jax moved deeper and deeper inside of me.

"Fuck baby, you're squeezing me so tight. If I were a normal man I wouldn't even make it all of the way inside of you before I blew." He pressed the pointed tip of his tail against my ass. "Lucky for you, I'm no weak mortal."

"If you think I waited nearly twenty-eight years for mediocre sex, you don't know me at all. If I was going to do it, I would only do it with the best. Lucky for me, I found it."

"Whose cock is it inside of you?" Jax demanded, finally shoving all the way in to where the tip of him brushed against my cervix. "Who owns this pussy?"

"You do, Jax. It's your pussy. Just like that's my cock I'm squeezing." I flexed my muscles, causing him to groan behind me. The hand in my hair released me to smack my ass.

"You're damn right it is." He gripped my hips with both hands. "Now, take this cock like a good girl."

He thrust into me hard. The edge of the island dug into my hips and legs. I didn't mind. The feeling of him so full and hard inside of me overrode any discomfort. We'd had all kinds of sex in the months since the first time. Some of which I hadn't even known was possible. But this was my favorite kind. The kind where the only thing that mattered was the feel of each other, the pleasure we could bring. The intensity was enough to have me sailing over the edge of pleasure into orgasm.

Normally, Jax would play with me. Keep me on the edge. Make me come again and again and again until I was begging him to stop. This time, he came with me. He allowed my orgasm to tug him into his own pleasure. I could feel the pulse and spurt of his cum inside of me as he gave himself over to it.

I loved that.

I loved that I could make this demon, designed and trained in pleasure and sex and lust, come for me. I loved it even more when he slowly slid out of me and helped me stand up. I loved the way he cared for me as he helped me clean his cum off my thighs before setting me back down to eat my cooling meal.

Sure, I might want a puppy for something to love. But I was loved so well, I could live without it. I couldn't live without the giant demon next to me.

***

"Fern, what the fuck?" I wasn't even out of the car before Jax was there, pulling open the door and swearing at me. Since he made it a point not to swear at me, I figured whatever had happened had rattled him.

"I'm going to need more context than 'what the fuck,' love." It didn't take long for the context to come.

The screen door flew open, and a giant black shape came barreling out. It bounded up to me and lunged. Jax was there to block the blow of it, but the large dog kept barking and fighting to get to me. His bark was deep, but he seemed happy enough, if you ignored the bright red eyes and spike-like tail.

"Hello there!" I said, petting its head. "Who is this?"

"Your fucking dog," Jax ground out. "The one you said you didn't need."

He apparently came to the same conclusion as me and decided the dog didn't intend to harm me. He stepped out of the way, and I found myself getting doggy kisses from the giant black beast.

"This is not a dog." I'd never had a dog before, but I knew enough about them to know that this was not your average man's best friend.

"Violet sent you a back to school gift. Meet your very own hellhound. Apparently, his name is Fluffy."

I couldn't help the laugh. I had mentioned to Violet that I wanted a dog and Jax's concern about them not liking demons. She told me there were hounds everywhere in her corner of Hell. I had not expected her to send me one. But it totally tracked she would send me a giant beast that looked like it would swallow a child whole and named it Fluffy.

"I swear to gods, I did not ask her for him." I got up and rested my hand on the hound's head. "I mean it. I don't need a dog. I can ask Violet to take him back."

"No, you can't." Jax sounded exhausted. At least he wasn't swearing at me anymore. "Once a hellhound bonds to their master, there's no reversing it. Violet bound him to you. You accepted him. The match is cemented. We're stuck with the beast."

We both looked down at the hound. Black as night, his coat was smooth and sleek. He sat on his hind legs with his tail thumping against the ground. His tongue lolled out of his mouth, which had too sharp of fangs for any normal breed. Flames danced in his red eyes. But despite the evil appearance, Fluffy seemed sweet.

"Aren't hellhounds evil?" We'd all done some reading on Hell lore and I was pretty sure I read that hellhounds were inherently evil.

"They can be. Fluffy seems mostly harmless." The dog snorted and fire flew out of his nostrils. Jax stomped on the grass to put the flames out. "I'm going to murder Violet."

"Shhh, no murder in front of the puppy." I covered the pointy ears on the dog's head and then scratched behind them. "I guess we need to go to the store. Wait, what do hellhounds eat?"

"You don't want to know," Jax grabbed my bag from the car and shouldered it before grabbing my hand and leading me into the house. "But don't worry, Violet sent us everything we'd need."

I patted my side, and Fluffy ran up to walk alongside us. I had to admit, the hound wasn't what I expected when I'd said I wanted a puppy. But he was oddly perfect for our weird little family.

"Are you angry?" I asked Jax, snuggling closer

to his side as we walked. While I was excited about the addition to our family, I knew Jax hadn't been interested in expanding. I know he said it was a permanent bond, but I would work with Violet to figure it out if he really wanted me to.

"Surprised, a little annoyed at her pushiness, but not mad and never at you." He stopped at the base of the steps and pressed a kiss to my head. "If the beast is what you want, we'll figure out how to make it work."

We both looked at the hound, who was sniffing around the bannister of the porch and the late summer flowers. He was definitely not the little terrier I'd imagined when I said I wanted a dog, but my heart already melted looking at the giant creature.

"Hey Jax."

"Yes, love?"

I grinned up at him, "I want an orgasm."

"Now this is one weird declarative statement I'm happy to accommodate." He scooped me up into a bridal carry and headed up the stairs. The big black dog followed us through the door, but seemed to understand not to follow when Jax took me up the stairs.

"Good dog," I told him, over Jax's shoulder. "Stay."

I probably just imagined the flare of flames in his eyes as we headed up the stairs.

Acknowledgments

Dear Reader, I'm going to be honest with you. When I wrote Corny it was as a hypo-manic joke following a conversation on Twitter about a very real bootylicious crochet candy corn (seriously, it's on Etsy). I expected maybe three people to read the book. No one was more shocked than I when people found it in the dark corners of the internet and read it. This book is for you. For every reader who read, reviewed, messaged me, and generally enjoyed the crazy world I created with that first story. It's for the community I've found since I started this mad journey, for the amazing, encouraging, welcoming readers and writers who enjoy the weirder side of romance.

Also to Josh, Amy, and Ellie - Thanks for listening to me talk about weird books and publishing even though I know you don't actually care beyond the fact it makes me happy. I couldn't do this life without you.

To Cate, Liz, Jae, NR, and all of the other writer friends I have made in the last few years. I'm so glad our corners of the internet met.

To Tay - I know you think I'm crazy and wonder when I fell off the deep end. Thanks for supporting me anyway.

To Cassie - Thanks for inviting me to the cool kids' table. And to everyone there, thank you for being so kind, welcoming, supportive, and generous with your time and knowledge.

To Mom - I cannot believe you're telling people I write this shit. Thanks for the support. I wouldn't be weird enough to write it if not for you.

To Dad - I can't believe you won't read my books. For shame.

To Brittany - Thanks for every late-night panic flail, talking me off many ledges, gassing me up, letting me ramble, and helping me find the plot when I get lost. For taking my word vomit and making it something worth reading. These books literally would not exist without you.

And to you, dear reader. Thanks for making it this far, for taking a chance on something a little unhinged, for every review, Instagram post, and encouraging comment. You're the reason I get to keep writing and doing something I love. Y'all are the best and I adore you.

About the Author

Sabrina Cross (she/her) is a neurospicy 80's baby from the middle of nowhere Michigan, where she still lives with her cat. She came into her monster romance era early when she fell in love with Beast from the 1997's X-Men animated series. After discovering sentient object romance in early 2023, Sabrina decided to embrace what she calls her 'Hold My Beer' style of writing and gave into the lifelong dream of being an author. When not writing weird monster/sentient object smut, Sabrina can be found hanging out on social media (@authorsabrinacross), reading, or hoarding office supplies.

Also by Sabrina Cross

Yarn & Monsters Series

A True Love Spell Gone Wrong...

When four friends perform a true love spell, things go terribly wrong. Now they're locked into a deal with the devil and have only a year to find love and happiness or their souls are destined to face the flames. Armed with a demon guardian; Clover, Jasmine, Fern, and Violet are determined to beat the devil and save themselves. Except, this curse might be the best thing that's ever happened to them.

Corny: A F/F Candy Corn Romance

A True Love Spell Gone Wrong...

A Demon Fairy Godmother?

Her very soul on the line. Can Clover still find true love or is she destined to face the flames alone?

Snuggle: A M/F Demon Teddy Bear Romance

A True Love Spell Gone Wrong...

Jasmine is too busy to go to Hell and she's definitely too busy for demon antics. But when her demon "Fairy Godmother" shows up, everything is on the line. Does she have what it takes to get out of the Devil's bargain or is she doomed to face the flames?

Tangled: A M/F Friends-To-Lovers Sentient Object Romance

A True Love Spell Gone Wrong...

Fern is going to Hell. Not metaphorical Hell but actual, physical Hell. But there's one thing she needs to do before she goes. An item she desperately needs to scratch off the bucket list. And she's hoping the demon sent to guard her will be willing to help her out.

Knotted: A M/F Demon Werewolf Romance

A True Love Spell Gone Wrong...

Violet was no witch but that didn't stop her from trying to use magic to find love. When the spell backfired and left her and her friends bound in a deal with the devil, Violet vowed to find a solution. Now, with less than two months until the deal comes due and zero leads, she's facing the fire. The fire comes early in the form of a great black beast in her bed. Does Violet find the love she's been looking for or does Hell claim her soul?

Light Me Up

He was the first man to ever turn me on. When he flipped my switch and lit me up that first time, I knew he was it for me. There would never be another.

Pounded by the Pommel Horse

Elena loves being on top. When the elite gymnast is challenged to defeat her gym rival on the pommel horse, she's up for the task. But is she up for the ride when the pommel horse shapeshifts into a man? A very, very naked Man?

Christmas with the Monster

He's Got a Package for Her... Devynn expected her first holiday without her kids to be difficult. But nothing could have prepared her for what she found under the tree just after midnight.With the help of his magic sack, the furry, green giant promises Devynn all kinds of pleasure. But would one night with the Christmas monster ever be enough?

Sentient Pen15 from Outer Space

Liam had spent a lot of his childhood obsessed with the legends of the local mines. The abandoned tunnels underground had driven dozens of workers insane and young Liam was desperate to get to the bottom of it. But he found more than he bargained for down there.

Infected by parasitic space mold, Liam has held himself away from relationships for years. When things spark between him and the girl next door, he has no choice but to reveal the truth: his manly appendage is also the bane of his existence.